SPIDER-MAN

Night of the Vulture!

By Frank J. Berrios
Illustrated by Francesco Legramandi and Silvano Scolari

 A GOLDEN BOOK • NEW YORK

© 2017 MARVEL marvelkids.com

randomhousekids.com
ISBN 978-1-5247-1728-5 (trade) — ISBN 978-1-5247-1729-2 (ebook)
Printed in the United States of America
10 9 8 7 6

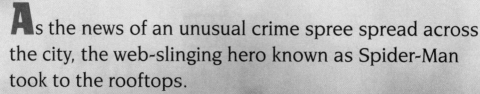

As the news of an unusual crime spree spread across the city, the web-slinging hero known as Spider-Man took to the rooftops.

This doesn't make sense, thought Spider-Man. *Several tech factories were broken into, all in one night. Who could be behind this? I'd better get to the scene of the crime.*

"No clues here," he mumbled as he swung away from the scene of the first robbery. "Maybe I'll have better luck at those other places uptown."

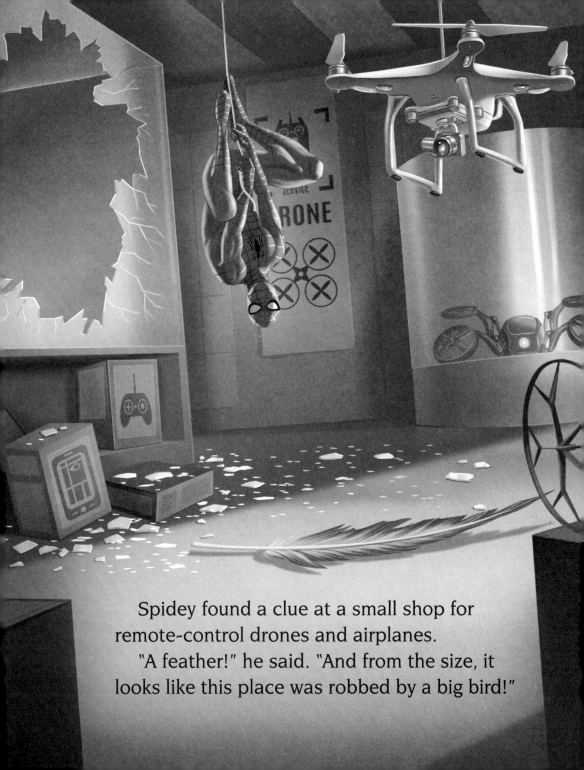

Spidey found a clue at a small shop for remote-control drones and airplanes.

"A feather!" he said. "And from the size, it looks like this place was robbed by a big bird!"

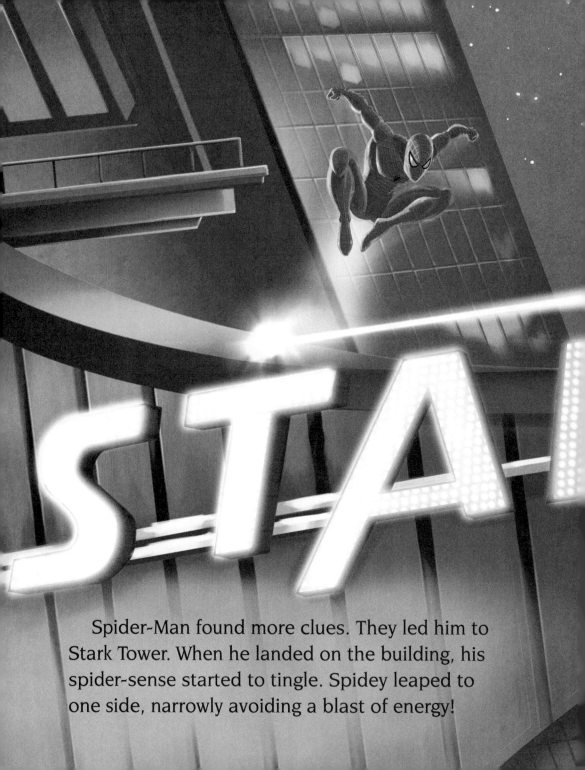

Spider-Man found more clues. They led him to Stark Tower. When he landed on the building, his spider-sense started to tingle. Spidey leaped to one side, narrowly avoiding a blast of energy!

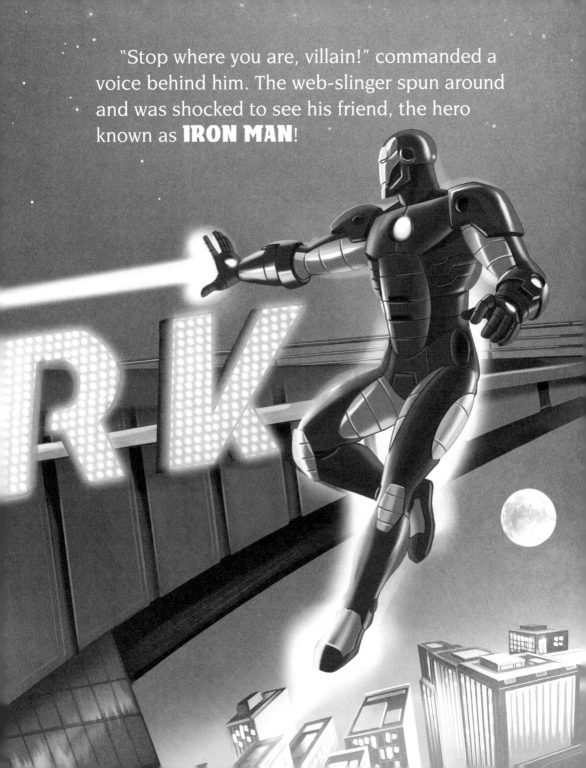

"Stop where you are, villain!" commanded a voice behind him. The web-slinger spun around and was shocked to see his friend, the hero known as **IRON MAN**!

"Apologies, Spider-Man. I thought you were the thief, trying to break into Stark Tower," said Iron Man.

"No worries, Shellhead," replied Spidey. "Is everything safe here?"

"Let's make sure," Iron Man replied.

Inside Stark Tower, the lights suddenly went out.

"I guess Mr. Stark forgot to pay the bills," joked Spidey.

"Someone has broken into Stark Tower," warned Iron Man, "and I think they're still here!"

"There!" whispered Iron Man. A bird-shaped drone sliced through the air and snatched Stark's top-secret Flight Technology plans. Iron Man fired his repulsor rays at the drone, but it slipped away.

"Blast that thing, Shellhead!" shouted Spidey as the drone shot down the hallway. "Before it gets out the window!"

"Too late!" replied Iron Man.

The heroes raced outside and were shocked to discover the villainous **Vulture**!

"Now all those tech-shop robberies make sense," exclaimed Spider-Man. "He was stealing tech for things that fly."

"Catch me if you can,
do-gooders!" said the Vulture.
"I have what I came for."

"Let's get that bad bird," said Spidey, "and get your tech plans back!"

"Deal," replied Iron Man.

The Vulture swooped down and swerved toward the park. He zipped over rocks, around trees, and under bridges to escape. But no matter how fast he flew, the villain couldn't get away from the two heroes.

"This will shake you off my tail feathers!" growled the Vulture, and he filled the air with more drones to distract the heroes.

"Until next time!" the Vulture cackled, making his getaway.

"I can't believe the Vulture escaped!" said Iron Man as Spider-Man finished off the last two drones. "With Stark's new Flight Technology, there's no telling what he'll do next!"

"Cool down, Shellhead! While you were busy blasting drones, I tossed one of my spider-tracers onto our flying foe," said Spidey. "Now all we have to do is follow him to his nest."

"**KNOCK-KNOCK!** Anybody home?" said
Spidey. He and Iron Man had followed the tracer to
an old skyscraper and snuck up on the Vulture.
The villain snarled, furious that he had been
followed. He dove out a window to escape!

The Vulture weaved through the city, racing toward a crowded tunnel.

"We can't let him get away again!" shouted Iron Man.

"Don't worry, Shellhead," Spidey said. "There's no light at the end of the tunnel for this flying fugitive!"

Just in the nick of time, Spider-Man covered
the tunnel entrance with webbing—**TWHICK!**
The fast-flying Vulture flew right into it.

"I guess things got a little sticky for the Vulture," Iron Man said.

"He'll be back in his cage soon enough!" Spider-Man replied as he handed the jailbird over to the police. "And that's just where he belongs."